The
Void

MAUREEN YOUNGER

DEDICATION

Für die Burschen.

CONTENTS

ACKNOWLEDGMENTS

To Jen Brister, Jayne Phenton and VG Lee for their unstinting assistance, support and patience. .

VIENNA

****

There is always a strange feeling when you go back to a city that was once your home. You know the city as it was, but not as it is. You think of your friends there as they once were and not as they have become and, more importantly, you think of yourself as you wished you had remained. In her case, that was young, carefree and with her life still ahead of her, unaware of all the possibilities and opportunities she would blithely disregard. Ignorant of all the time she would waste. All the time she was still wasting.

It was as if she'd left a life there she could have lived and now she was back; the city and the people had moved on, and everything was just ever so slightly out of sync.

These thoughts scurried through her mind as she looked around Vienna's West Station and felt something was amiss and not just the fact that he hadn't turned up to meet her as promised. After thirty years he could have been on time or at least sent a text to say where he was.

Nevertheless, she continued to look around the station hoping against hope that he was there. West Station. She couldn't remember exactly how it looked when she'd first come to Vienna in 1984, but it certainly had never looked like this nor had it been so spacious. Now it merely seemed to be another excuse for a shopping centre.

As if to reassure herself that some things never change, she ignored the numerous modern eateries on offer and headed across the road, rolling her suitcase behind her, across one side of the ring road, appropriately called the Gürtel, the German for belt, over the jumble of tram tracks, over the other side of the Gürtel, to a coffee house in the traditional Viennese style; just how she liked it. She plopped herself down and as soon as the waitress scuttled over, she asked for a melange, her coffee of choice. Minutes later the waitress was back, the melange on a silver tray accompanied by the obligatory glass of water; Austrian style.

She sent off a text telling him where she was and got out her book, an all-time favourite, pacing herself with her coffee as she pretended to read. It was hard to concentrate. She might be looking at the words, but she was thinking of him. Trust him to be late. Maybe some things don't change after all. His unreliability; her stupidity.

2

She poked around in her handbag, dumping several bits and pieces of its contents next to her coffee on the table, when she finally found what she was looking for: her mirror. She then stuffed the miscellaneous items back into her bag, and snapped the mirror open and looked at her face. Yes, some things do change. She was losing her looks; she had gained weight. That was evident as she stroked the layer of fat under her chin. She raised the mirror higher for a more flattering look: well, at least her cheekbones were still hanging in there. As for her hair, it still refused to adhere to any recognisable hairstyle and up close the brown tint was probably a bit too dark to go with the face. She let out a loud sigh and placed the mirror back in the bag.

Perhaps she should contact another friend in the city, surprise them with her arrival; hint about whether she could stay with them. She had said nothing about her visit to anyone else, feeling embarrassed by the whole affair. Affair - that was an odd choice of words. Their so-called affair thirty years ago had been such an unmitigated disaster, it seemed inaccurate to call it one. So why was she here now?

She looked at her phone. Still no bloody text. She rang, but the phone went straight to voicemail. She had a choice. She could sit here, waiting for him to get in touch and pretend to read her book, or do something. Her natural inclination was to check out some of her old haunts.

In the old days whenever she'd felt at a loss, she would walk from the Josefstadt, where she shared a flat opposite his, to Schönbrunn Palace and walk up the hill to the Gloriette. It was a hell of a walk, but it gave her some kind of aim whenever she was feeling particularly aimless. And she always felt aimless whenever her non-relationship with him had hit an impasse, which was often. Being mid-winter, it was freezing, her nose would go bright red in the cold and it was tiring walking through all that snow and sludge. Somehow the physical exertion helped alleviate the emotional turmoil going on inside her. She'd get to the top of the hill, crowned by The Gloriette, panting as if she were in dire need of oxygen, and survey the formal gardens, covered in snow, leading to the yellow palace below, Austria's answer to Versailles. The very fact she had managed to reach the heady climes of the Gloriette felt like some kind of achievement against the failure of her non-existent love life.

Thirty years on, she decided she'd forget the walking there part and take the tram, at least that way she'd still get to see something of the city. She paid for her melange and trundled back over the Gürtel and tramlines. Having stored her suitcase in one of the lockers at the station, she splashed out on a day ticket and headed for the 58 tram stop. Only to find that like the J-Wagen before it, it had been replaced and she needed the 65. Yet another reminder that she was now out of sync with a city she had once considered home. Minutes later a tram arrived and she jumped on board, looking intently out the windows as the tram sped along.

Once at Schönbrunn, she walked through the gardens and headed straight for the Gloriette. Panting her way to the top again, as in days of yore, having to stop once or twice to get her breath back, she finally stood underneath it, looking down at the summer palace of the Hapsburgs. It was a spectacular memorial to an Empire that no longer existed; a country that had once stretched from the Netherlands to Northern Italy and as far east as parts of present-day Ukraine, and which had been truncated to its German-speaking rump after the First World War. The Empire might be long gone, but Vienna's cornucopia of over-the-top buildings were a visible reminder of the city's imperial past: they were just a bit too big, just a bit too impressive for a country of its size and importance. Like her, they were out of sync with reality. Maybe she was more at home here than she realised.

She stared at the Palace and wondered how much she had changed since she used to come here as a student. She'd come to Vienna originally to study German and Russian. She had duly enrolled as a foreign student at Vienna's grand university, once she had managed to work her way through the maze of Austrian bureaucracy.

This early brush with Austrian officialdom had made her appreciate why Kafka had written the stories he had. As a foreign student you had to register separately from everyone else at the university. She would queue up, hand in her papers, only to be told by a bored admin assistant, 'Ihnen fehlt was'. Evidently, she was missing something, but the admin assistant would never tell her, as a matter of principle, what the thing was that was missing. She'd finally track down what she suspected was the problem, correct it, and with renewed hope she would return to the university and queue back up again, only to be told 'Ihnen fehlt was'.

She soon learnt it was seemingly a deeply-held principle of the country's officialdom that Austrian bureaucrats never told you all the things that were missing in one fell swoop, but rather preferred a more drip-feed approach. That way things took longer, you wasted more time and they had more opportunity to tell you your papers were incorrect. Things improved appreciably once a kind-hearted Austrian took pity on her and explained what a Trafik and Bundesstempelmarken were, both words that had never featured in any of the German she'd learnt over the years. A Trafik, it turned out, was the Austrian for tobacconists. These small shops were dotted all over Vienna and had a handy side line selling tickets and travel cards as well as stamps, which is where the phenomenon of Bundesstempelmarken came in. In the mid-1980s at least, it seemed as if Austrian officialdom was unable to process any paperwork unless a Bundesstempelmarke or two was attached to it.

Finally, she was enrolled and after all that bureaucratic kerfuffle she attended the odd lecture and wisely decided she would learn more German by socialising with Austrians. This proved to be true, although it did little to improve her Russian. It was then she got to know him, in the Café Hummel in the Josefstadt, where in hindsight she realised she'd spent some of the happiest evenings of her youth.

1984: it all seemed a hell of a long time ago and yet it seemed like yesterday. What did she have to show for all those intervening years? Not much. More to the point, why in heaven's name was she still so attached to a city she'd lived in for a mere six months over thirty years ago?

Why had she turned up here to meet someone she'd never really been in a proper relationship with, although at the time she had convinced herself that this was "it" – the grand romance?

There is something addictive about unrequited love. It can last for years, every rejection feeding your habit, placing you firmly in the crosshair between low self-esteem and self-delusion. Convinced that if only the object of your affection would realise how right *you* were for *them,* then how happy *they* would be. If only they knew how much you loved them, surely, they would fall at your feet. Often, it's the fact that *you* don't know *them* which helps fuel the addiction. Unrequited love works best when the beloved doesn't live anywhere near you, preferably abroad and above all else is emotionally unavailable, at least to you.

Obviously, you refuse to accept they are emotionally unavailable through self-deception, misunderstanding and sheer persistence. It's easy. Whenever they say something you don't want to hear, you tell yourself they mean the opposite. He doesn't want a girlfriend? As far as you're concerned, what he's really saying is that he doesn't want a girlfriend *apart* from you. The truth? He wouldn't mind a girlfriend, just *not* you!

Why do this to ourselves? Is it self-hate? Is it fear? Have we set ourselves impossible ideals to such an extent that a non-relationship suits our needs much better than an actual relationship, subject to all its faults and failures?

'Oh, Christ,' she thought. This was too much internalising. She would concentrate on something far more palpable. Feeling hungry, she made her way to a restaurant she knew.

It wasn't that close. A good 20-minute walk at least, but she needed to keep busy. It was packed as usual, but there was still one empty table outside at the back so she made her way over, rushing slightly in case some new diner entered and beat her to it. She glanced at the menu, but already knew what she was going to order. The same thing she always ordered: goulash and bread dumplings.

A few minutes after ordering her meal, and once more pretending to be engrossed in her book, she heard a male voice from above summon her attention. For a fleeting moment she thought it might be him, but it couldn't be. He didn't know she was here. She looked up to see a young man, flashing a bright set of white teeth as he smiled down at her.

'May I?' he asked in German as he pointed to the bench opposite hers, and then looked round at the busy tavern as if to say this was the only room in the inn.

'Ja, sicher,' she replied and smiled back. He was a good-looking bloke, tall, fine featured, olive skin with a mop of curly black hair she quickly noted. She closed her book, having decided she would engage him in conversation. Despite all recent proof to the contrary, in her head she sometimes still saw herself as the foxy young thing she'd been in her twenties, and unable to help herself, she began to flirt.

Fortunately the young man, Agustín, mistook her flirting for simple friendliness; the kind of immediate friendship that two foreigners strike up when meeting in a foreign land.

She soon learnt he was from Mexico, 24 years old, happily engaged to an Austrian which was how he had ended up working in Lambach in Upper Austria where the hardest part of his job was trying to understand the local dialect. She commiserated with him, and they talked about Austria, Vienna, what an idiot the American president was and how, if he liked great countryside, Agustín should visit Scotland.

It was only when they were sipping their coffees, she another melange, he an espresso, it hit her that the conversation they were having was like the conversations she used to have when she was a student in Vienna. Neither had looked at their phone, checked their social media or taken a call. They had spent an hour and a half conversing and enjoying each other's company.

It also hit her she hadn't once thought of him, he that must not be named, he who had been supposed to meet her almost three hours ago. She hadn't even checked if he'd been in touch. At the thought, she immediately looked at her phone. He hadn't.

As for Agustín, she was aware by now that flirt all she might, he was far too young and she far too old to be regarded as a sexual object by him. This realisation didn't bother her. She recalled how she had been hit on enough times when she was younger by much older men to appreciate it wasn't rejection per se it was just life. And, anyway, she was simply enjoying his company, he was making her laugh and she needed that.

He looked at his watch. 'I need to go into town,' he replied in his American-accented English. They had soon abandoned speaking German once Maureen mentioned she was British.

'Oh of course,' she replied, not quite able to hide the disappointment in her voice.

'I have to meet some friends,' he explained. He hesitated for a moment and catching the waiter's eye, signalled for the bill. Then, turning back towards her, he asked, 'Would you like to come? Or maybe you already have plans?'

'No plans,' she immediately replied and switched off her phone, without even checking the screen, and stuffed it into her handbag.

A few minutes later, having paid, following a rather lengthy discussion of how much tip one should leave (she took a more European view, he more of an American one) they got up to go.

'Your book," Agustín pointed to a well-thumbed copy of Stefan Zweig's A Letter from an Unknown Woman, lying on the table by the empty coffee cup.

She shook her head and scrunched up her nose. 'It's fine. Leave it for someone else.'

'You finished it?' Agustín asked.

'In a way,' she smiled, 'I suppose I have'.

.

THE NIGHTIE

She hadn't bought a new outfit in years. Walking into her bedroom, this was hard to believe. Two wardrobes in the tiny room were crammed with clothes. Under her bed lay several suitcases, stuffed with even more garments; each one charting her adulthood and the corresponding increase in dress size. A decade ago she had stopped buying clothes all together, refusing to admit she now needed a size 20. Instead, one by one, the number of clothes she could wear from among her humongous wardrobe had dwindled down to the half dozen or so dresses she could still squeeze into. Thank God for polyester! She told herself that if she didn't buy any clothes, she wouldn't have to admit that she had crossed the Rubicon: size 20 was just one size too far. She had compensated by buying accessories – any size fits after all. Well, apart from bangles.

At times she found it hard to believe that in her youth she had been a size 10 and had possessed a slim figure which she had never appreciated at the time. But from her mid-30s the pounds had accrued gradually and inexorably; month in month out. It was always the same. Every time she reached a weight milestone, she would do a double take. By her mid-30s, she weighed 12 stone and told herself she must lose weight. She didn't. The weight continued to creep up. As she neared her 40th birthday, she tipped the scales at 13 stone. Once more, she said to herself, enough was enough, but it turned out it wasn't, and on the eve of her 50th birthday, she had reached the giddy heights of 16 stone. That really was enough. She envisaged herself being 'featured' on one of those reality TV programmes, something along the lines of '28 Stone Woman Crushed to Death by Her Accessories'. It was time to do the unthinkable and eat healthily!

Until this point, she had remained in denial, aided and abetted by her female friends who were always very supportive when it came to her weight. As a rule, female friends are always supportive - at least to your face. Behind your back the general consensus may be somewhat different. Outwardly, at least, her friends were reassuring and adamant that she didn't look her weight. After all, she was very tall. In reality she wasn't that tall. For someone of her weight, she figured she would probably need to be 9 foot 8 and she was pretty certain, if memory served her right, that at best she was 5 foot 7.

As a child of the 70s - well technically the 60s and the 70s (but she was in denial about her age too) - she had grown up with all the unhealthy eating peccadillos innate to that era. It was an age which embraced the avid consumption of such healthy delights as crispy pancakes, garlic bread and sweets disguised as cigarettes. Then there were the special nights out at a Wimpy. These would invariably include chicken nuggets, chips and, to top the night off in style, a Knickerbocker Glory.

Added to that, despite living in North London, she had grown up in an inveterate Scottish working-class family. This meant that no meal was complete without a considerable amount of high-saturated fat, and where preferably at least one item on the plate – if not all - had been fried. As a child, her biggest culinary treat was when her dad cooked potato fritters for supper.

In those days, among her family at least, the main aim of cooking seemed to be to eliminate any nutritional value the food might possibly contain. True, dessert often consisted of fruit, but always out of a tin, either mandarin segments, pear pieces or if mum was in a particularly exotic mood, fruit cocktail; any nutritional value which might have survived the canning process was then counterbalanced either with ice cream, custard or evaporated milk.

For the last 10 days, however, she had been good and eaten salads, gone out walking and denied herself her usual four cups of coffee a day. As a result, she had lost a whopping five lbs. She conceded it didn't make her Kate Moss, but she was now down to 15 stone 9 and was already imagining the possibility of having the figure she used to have when she was in her early 30s and still a desirable, young woman.

To celebrate surviving 10 days of not eating chocolate, drinking caffeine and late-night eating, she decided to treat herself to a new nightie. Her current set of pyjamas had definitely seen better days. The back of the trousers sported a cluster of holes of varying sizes and shapes. By anybody's reckoning not the sexiest of looks. She had been single since the heady days of being a size 14 but she now resolved to go back to her former sexy self and to invest in some decent and enticing nightwear.

This proved a more difficult shop than she had imagined. She quickly realised certain shops weren't for her. Much to her annoyance one shop didn't even size the clothes, but just labelled them small, medium and large. She made her way to the counter and asked the shop assistant what size was a large. '12,' the woman replied. 'What?' she asked incredulously. 'A large is a size 12,' the assistant confirmed. 'Not in Britain,' she assured her. 'Have you been down the High Street recently? I think you'll find that to the average Brit a size 12 is wishful thinking.' The shop assistant stared at her blankly.

It was apparent that when it came to buying a nightdress her only options seemed to be between dressing like her grandmother or dressing like a slut. She planned on putting off the former for as long as possible. As for the slut option, she might be down to 15 stone 9, but she knew that still didn't mean she'd look good in a see-through, nylon, baby doll nightie with accompanying frilly, see-through G-string knickers. And then there was the comfort aspect. 'Who the hell would want to wear a pair of G-string knickers to bed?' she thought to herself. 'Who the hell would want to wear a pair of G-string knickers full stop?' She'd never understood the attraction. She tried them a couple of times and found them literally bumnumbingly excruciating. So what if people saw your panty line? It just proved you were wearing knickers. Surely that was a good thing, wasn't it?

Then in what seemed like the zillionth shop of the afternoon, and on the verge of giving up, there it was, hanging in front of her, as she wandered into the lingerie department. A lovely black nightie, fringed with cream lace and even better, hidden breast support. She wasn't exactly sure what that was, but it sounded good. What more could you want? 'Hopefully my size!' she said to herself. She couldn't believe her luck. Her size was there. She grabbed the nightie as well as one in the next size down – just in case. 'Well, you never know,' she thought to herself, 'I have lost 5 lbs after all.'

Her luck definitely was in. There was no queue outside the dressing room. There was, however, a gaggle of shop assistants gathered at the entrance, clearly resenting the arrival of a customer interrupting their private and rather lively conversation. Begrudgingly a young Asian girl wearing a headscarf and ensconced in copious amounts of make-up sauntered over.

'Sorry, I didn't see you there,' the shop assistant said as she took the nighties from her, and after counting the two items, handed them back to her along with an electronic tag. 'Dressing room three,' the shop assistant announced and sauntered back to her colleagues. Having taken the proffered tag from the shop assistant, she stared at the two rows of empty dressing rooms, banked against the walls, puzzled as to why the shop assistant was so adamant that she should use that particular dressing room.

Nonetheless she went into the allocated dressing room, closed the curtain behind her and started to undress. Staring at herself in the full-length mirror, she had to admit it wasn't a great look, standing there in mismatched knickers and bra, her stomach spilling over in waves around her midriff. She slipped on the nightie in the larger size and immediately felt better about herself. The nightie's A-line shape skimmed her stomach and flattered her silhouette. The hidden breast support pulled her breasts together and gave them shape. Then she tried the smaller size.

Admittedly, deep down she had suspected that although she might technically be able to fit into the smaller size, it probably wouldn't be as flattering. And she had suspected correctly. This one didn't skim her body like the previous one. Her various stomachs rippled through the material. She quickly undressed again, put the larger size back on and confirmed what she already knew. 'Maybe next time,' she thought to herself, glancing at the discarded smaller version lying on the floor by her feet. She took the larger nightie off again and hung it carefully back on to the hanger. She checked the price. £19.50! Her luck really was holding out. The nightie was even reasonably priced.

Not believing her good fortune, she rushed to the cash desk. Once there, she saw with horror that her luck had now taken a turn for the worse. There were three people queuing up ahead of her wanting to return various items. Under normal circumstances she would swear under her breath, dump her intended purchase down at the nearest opportunity and flounce out of the shop.

However, this was the first piece of clothing she had wanted to buy in 10 years and so, contrary to her natural inclinations towards extreme impatience – she was a Londoner after all - she waited in line with gritted teeth while the next person ahead of her emptied their plastic carrier bag full of returned goods.

It seemed that although each customer had a cornucopia of items to bring back, none of them had bothered to bring back the one thing they really needed - their receipts. The process was clearly going to take some time. She continued to grit her teeth, play with her mobile phone - despite not having any signal - until finally it was her turn.

The cashier took the nightie, looked her up and down as if she were asking herself why someone like her would want to buy something so nice and then tried to persuade her to get a credit card. 'I live abroad,' she replied. She didn't but it shut up the shop assistant once and for all. She took £20 from her purse, which for the most part was bulging with receipts and vouchers that she would never use, and handed the note over to the cashier.

Once home, she was tempted to place her lovely new purchase where so many lovely new purchases of lingerie and nightwear had gone before – destined never to be worn. The lingerie graveyard that was her bottom drawer. There she kept all her sexy underwear in various sizes and colours, bought for that special romantic occasion which never came: sexy silk French knickers and matching tops, the odd sexy teddy from the early 90s.

She had once taken a set of black silk French

knickers and matching top for a trip to the Lake District with a new boyfriend. It was their first romantic weekend away together and, as it transpired, their last. The new (and soon to be ex) boyfriend unilaterally decided to spend their first supposedly amorous night together engrossed in watching Match of the Day. In response, she unilaterally decided that to put the sexy lingerie on would be a complete waste of time. Thus, despite the best of intentions, the outfit never got an airing. The said items swiftly went back into her suitcase and from there straight back to their inevitable final resting place in the graveyard that was her lingerie drawer.

She wasn't quite sure why she insisted on keeping all these forlorn reminders of romantic wishful thinking from her past. It wasn't as if she could ever wear them, even in the unlikely event an opportunity arose where they would be required. Not only would her love life have to take a serious turn for the better, she'd also have to lose several stone or suddenly become the victim of a virulent wasting disease for them to fit.

She opened the drawer and looked at the various silken underwear before her - never worn and, more importantly, never taken off. She thought of all the almost-romances that marked her life, of the men she had spent years obsessing about to little avail and who, looking back, she now realised had, from the first, clearly not been that interested in her, if only she'd been prepared to admit it at the time. Her ability to delude herself, to read signs of hope where none existed and her dogged desire to be "understanding" in the face of general indifference belied her natural intelligence.

She then thought of the admirers she had either been indifferent to or whose overtures at the time she had been blithely unaware of. Yes, she conceded, for an intelligent woman she couldn't half be an idiot when it came to matters of the heart.

She remembered how her greatest fear as a young child was to end up like the mad, old lady she sometimes used to see on the No 16 bus. The woman, made up to the nines, but obviously lonely, would ride the No 16 bus all day, talking to strangers in the way that only truly lonely people do, talking non-stop, desperate to be in a conversation with another human being, with someone, anyone. Her sheer desperate need to converse would ensure that no one wanted to talk to her. People would do their very best to avoid the old lady, including her. Even as a small child she could sense the loneliness and desperation that engulfed this woman. She had prayed that she would not end up like her, but as she looked at the sea of multi-coloured silk in front of her, she reflected that her greatest fear was likely to come true. After all, her romantic life had not been that fantastic when she had been young and sexy. What were the chances now as a 50 something - albeit 5 lbs lighter than she had been 10 days before?

She thought of the men who she was still friends with and with whom at some point or other something might have happened, but in the end, nothing ever had. She conceded she had screwed up big time on at least a couple of occasions, when she had met men who, she realised in hindsight, would have been ideal for her. She had let these opportunities sail by, having no idea of how rare and valuable they were. 30 years on and there was definitely no going back.

Still sitting on her bed, clutching her new purchase, she thought of her friends who had found someone. Like a lot of women, she thought the majority of her friends could have done a lot better than the person they had ended up with. She was convinced they had settled. She couldn't tell them this of course. What would be the point? Even if they broke up with the said individual, she still couldn't say anything - just in case they got back with them. She'd learned that valuable lesson in her 20s when, elated at her then best friend breaking up with her long-term boyfriend, she had finally told her what she really thought of him. Needless to say, her friend got back with her boyfriend soon afterwards, told him what she had said about him and that was the end of that particular friendship.

She too had tried to settle in her early-30s. It turned out to be her longest lasting relationship. It had lasted all of 15 months. Yes, 15 months had been the longest a relationship of hers had ever lasted. It seemed a rather pathetically short amount of time given the years she had been alive. She had been well aware at the time that she was settling, but she felt empowered because deep down she didn't care. But it had come with a price and the price was that the relationship had numbed her soul. Then as soon as he suggested they move in together into his flat in South London, she promptly moved to Glasgow. Anyone who would rather move to a city over 400 miles away than move in with their boyfriend definitely had commitment issues. A month later they had split up, although that had been his idea.

When he'd suggested they break up, she'd nonchalantly replied: 'OK then'. The truth of the matter was she wasn't that bothered. She definitely didn't love him. She wasn't even sure she liked him. She suspected she had never liked him. What she had liked was the idea of having a boyfriend for once; that was what she had been more enamoured with rather than the reality of her relationship with him.

Having agreed that they should break up, she remembered putting down the phone and thinking she'd better cry. She was sure that was the correct response. She went into her bedroom and decided to cry for three songs. She reckoned that was the commensurate number of tunes for a 15-month relationship. She put on a tape of slow 80s love tunes – surely a safe choice – but half way through the first song she realised she couldn't be arsed.

She got up off the bed where she'd flung herself in a fit of supposed dramatic pique. She went into the kitchen and made herself a coffee and a cheese sandwich and turned on the portable TV. For the next couple of hours, she sat engrossed as she watched the omnibus episode of a particularly awful American soap opera. So awful that she couldn't help but watch it. It was like a bad car accident you drive past on the motorway. You know you shouldn't look but you just can't seem to tear yourself away.

Mulling all this over, she got up and went to put the nightie in the lingerie graveyard drawer. Then she remembered the one guy whom she had met, loved and

lost and who – despite 20 years after their brief romance –
she was still friends with. She thought how distraught she
had been when the romance had died - though it had died
a lot earlier than she had realised at the time; nine months
before to be exact. When the penny finally dropped, she
had felt as if she had been given everything she could ever
want in a man only for it to be snatched away from her.
She thought too about how he had never actually loved
her despite finding her compelling and sexy. And then she
remembered how needy she had been and, truthfully, she
couldn't really blame him.

What were her options now? Men who thought
that at her age and size she should just be grateful. She
wasn't. Men who had clearly been with too many women
with low self-esteem and as a result thought they could
treat her accordingly. They couldn't. Married men who
thought she would be up for being a bit on the side. No
thanks. And recently an aging intellectual who had
buckets full of charm, but the emotional make up of an
insecure, spotty teenager.

The final straw was when he brought another
woman along with him the last time they met up, and then
seemed rather uncomfortable when she didn't seem elated
at the prospect. Afterwards he had emailed her to
apologise for behaving so badly and to let her know that
the evening had been very unpleasant for him. In other
words, he'd emailed her in order to apologise to himself.
Strangely enough, they were no longer in touch.

She knew she had to do something to ensure that
the nightie didn't end up suffering the same fate as all the

sexy lingerie that had gone before it. Whilst pondering how exactly she was going to solve that little conundrum, she quickly undressed, slipped on the nightie and sat down on the edge of the bed. 'I'm not sure this counts,' she muttered to herself.

There comes a point in every woman's life when you become invisible to the opposite sex. Men stop paying attention to you, stop looking at you in that certain way, stop volunteering to do things for you or even stop noticing that you are there. When she was young, she hadn't appreciated the innate power she had as an attractive, young woman. Men had always been helpful and attentive. It happened so often that she assumed it was normal. It seemed so entirely natural that she didn't even question it. Then as the years passed it began to stop.

When it first started happening, she thought it was amusing. Then slowly her intrinsic power as an attractive woman dissipated almost completely and it threw her for six. The men she knew in her 20s still treated her as the sexy, young woman she had been. After all they still saw her, the real her, the her she still felt herself to be and not the middle-aged woman she'd become. However, in general, she had become transparent and this indifference ate away at her soul.

Yes, she had got older and the pounds had piled on, but she still believed herself to be the intelligent, witty and vivacious woman she had always considered herself to be. That hadn't changed, had it? The essential her was still there. Or had she been mistaken all that time? Maybe she hadn't been as interesting as she'd always imagined. Maybe people hadn't been attracted to what she perceived to be her quick wit and quick mind. Maybe people had simply indulged her because they found her attractive and shagable.

As she grew older, she noticed not only how invisible she was becoming but how middle-aged women seem to disappear from all aspects of society – from literature, from TV, from films, apparently not even allowed to read the news on TV. Of course, there were the odd exceptions where older women were allowed to make a fleeting appearance on screen: if they were personifying the interfering mother, the moaning ex-wife, the aged prostitute (invariably with a heart of gold), the doddering grand-mother, but in the main – unless they were Helen Mirren, Judi Dench or Maggie Smith - older women in TV and films were reduced to bit parts.

No wonder Sex and the City had been such a big success. It was one of the few programmes which featured women over 35 who weren't just someone's mother or embittered ex. Admittedly, her life was nothing like theirs. She never faced the horrendous quandary of having a limitless designer wardrobe or having to choose between two hot men such as Big and Aidan, but at least Carrie, Miranda, Charlotte and Samantha were more or less in the same age bracket as her.

While the programme had been running, she had always identified with Miranda, but what if she was more like Samantha in that deep down she never wanted to be in a relationship. Yes, she wanted love, she wanted sex, she wanted affection, but did she want to be in a relationship?

With the odd exception, whenever she visited her friends who were in long-term relationships, she tended to feel a sense of relief that she was not in their predicament. So much so that at times when she felt really down about her dogged single status, she would visit certain friends in long-term relationships just to cheer herself up, and remind herself that at least she had standards. After all, being alone in a relationship is a lot lonelier than being alone per se.

Yes, she had friends who were in happy relationships, but she pitied those whose partners seemed to delight in chipping away at their self-esteem, in belittling them, and to some extent controlling them. She knew she would never have been willing to pay that high a price for a relationship and children. Perhaps there were women out there who felt it was a price worth paying to nest: putting up with men who would day-by-day tear them down bit-by-bit. Needless to say, she rubbed such men up the wrong way simply by existing. Moreover, she would commit the worst sin a woman could make in their eyes – she refused to pander to their egos to make them feel better about themselves.

It dawned on her that all things considered, maybe her personality didn't suit being in a relationship. She knew that the idea of checking in with someone before doing anything appalled her even though she understood why couples did it. Even as a temp, she'd never ask permission before she did anything. She would simply tell her bosses what she was doing, whether it was to say she needed a day off or that she'd be late coming in. She reasoned that if you tell someone, rather than ask them, then they can't say no.

She recalled going to the cinema on a date with a guy who she had been totally enamoured with. Ironically, he was now openly gay. So much for her Gaydar. She couldn't believe her luck. She was spending the whole evening with him. They arrived at the cinema and, as it so happened, he wanted to see one film; she had wanted to see another. Without a moment's hesitation, she had blithely said: 'Well you go and see what you want to see and I'll go and see my film and then I'll meet you in the foyer afterwards.' Needless to say, there had been no second date.

She concluded that with that independence of mind (it sounded much better than selfishness or lack of consideration of others) maybe she wasn't cut out to be in a relationship after all. Even she would find it difficult to go out with someone like her and she understood where she was coming from! She was too old to start a family and she couldn't see any budding relationships happening anytime soon. What could she do with her life? Make the most of it, she decided. Read, travel, catch up with friends, write?

She had spent most of her life on hold – waiting for something to happen, that great work opportunity to appear, the love of her life to turn up, that one event which was going to turn her life around. And while she waited, most of her life had passed her by. Her ability to procrastinate and waste time was second to none. She would spend days, months, even years agonising over a decision and then always make the wrong choice. Surely, she could make the wrong choice a lot quicker?

'Christ,' the thought struck her. 'How much time have I wasted thinking about this bleeding nightie?' She went next door and got her Notebook. Returning to the bedroom, she crawled on to the bed and switched the Notebook on, banging her head against the headboard several times as it took an age to come to life. She thought to herself. 'Bloody start writing. Something. But write about what?' She looked down at her nightie and began to type.

THE VOID

The one thing you can't seem to escape as a performer is the void. It's always there, looming in the background, ready to swallow you up. At times it seems to dissipate, disappear and you think you've outrun it, buried it, lost it but it always comes back, threatening to swallow you up.

It often unfolds itself at the least expected moments, tripping you up when you should be at your happiest – after a great performance, after a great gig, after a career milestone. For days, months, years you've been telling yourself if only I get that role, play that club, get that gig, it – whatever it is – will be different: I'll be successful, I'll be respected by my peers, I'll get more work, I'll be rich. What you're really telling yourself is: I'll be happy.

Maybe you get that role, play that club, get that gig, maybe it goes well, maybe it doesn't, maybe it just goes OK, maybe it goes better than expected: whatever the outcome the void is still there and you're still not happy. If anything, the void is looming larger than before because it dawns on you yet again that that role, that club, that gig wasn't the panacea to your unhappiness, your loneliness, your fears. But you have no idea what else to do – dealing with what really makes you unhappy seems far more scary - so you carry on thinking that the next role you get, club you play, gig you smash will definitely make the difference.

A skilled comic has the power – and it is power - of ripping the room apart, all that laughter because of you, everyone hanging on your every word, your every facial expression, every well-judged pause, every ad lib that you've said a hundred times before; people coming up and telling you how amazing you were (and if you're a female comedian someone – and that someone is usually another woman - assuring you they found you funny even though they don't normally like female comedians) and then you're on the bus/tube/in the car homewards, often on your own, alone, and you've dissolved into nothing again. The people who thought you were wonderful, amazing, hilarious and were hanging on your every word just a mere half an hour ago have already started to forget you; you're simply a footnote in their night out; at most, you're hazily remembered as that funny comic they saw one night whose name they can't remember.

As a comic your art, your skill at making a room full of strangers enter into whatever world you create and getting them to laugh, is ephemeral. Gone as soon as you say the words. A comic is only as good as their last gig the saying goes and it's true. You can rip it one night and then have a room full of strangers stare at you in complete disdain the next. No one is bulletproof. Every comic has died and every comic knows that somewhere along the line – no matter how good they are, how skilled, how well-written their jokes, how good their banter, they will die again. The better you are, the more consistent you are, the less often it will happen but it will happen. Maybe it's that fear which keeps the bigger fears at bay.

It's ironic that people who deep-down fear rejection, insist on putting themselves in a position where invariably they won't just be rejected by one person but rather by a whole room of people. In comedy, when you have a bad gig, it's not that the audience don't like your act, they invariably don't like YOU. It's not theatre; you can't hide behind the underwritten role, the out-of-depth director, the badly-written play: it's YOU, YOUR persona, YOUR words, confirming what you have always feared the most – that you're unlikeable and all those school bullies from years ago were right.

Then there is the rejection from promoters and bookers – some of whom would seem to know almost nothing about comedy but do enjoy the power they wield over their particular comedy empire. The constant knocking on doors which refuse to open even when you've done well all helps feed the void. After a while, your imagination starts working overtime and you begin to believe it's personal; you imagine that there is some big conspiracy to thwart your career as if bookers and promoters would seriously devote time and effort in stymieing you; but it's a far more tempting theory than the rather more prosaic if more likely reason that you're just another email in their inbox.

Fear of contacting promoters; fear of being rejected out-of-hand; of being ignored; passed over; the fear of silence, it all helps build that void. Perhaps most scarily of all, for someone who lives from their words is the void you feel when you come to write and you can't think of anything; you mind is a blank page so you try and fill that void by cleaning out the fridge, clearing out the shed, eating crap food, engaging in social media, watching some shite telly, anything to keep the void at bay, besides the one thing that might help solve it – to write.

When the void hits, it can make you realise what you've been running away from – love, affection, family, friends, sex, human companionship or perhaps more accurately the lack of them. For a job which exclusively has you in the centre of an ever-changing vortex of social situations, at heart the comic is always alone, and never more so when the void is about to envelop you.

ABOUT THE AUTHOR

Maureen Younger is a comedian, writer, actor and polyglot, having previously lived in Austria, Russia, Ukraine, Spain, France and Germany. As a stand up comedian, she has performed throughout the UK and abroad and has occasionally performed stand up in both German and French. As an actor, roles range from appearing as an angry German housewife in Band of Brothers on TV to appearing in the play Roger and Miriam as Miriam, an alcoholic, Jewish, New Yorker with a gay son. Maureen has also written articles for various magazines. This is her first collection of short stories. For more information, please head to www.maureenyounger.com/ @maureenyounger.

Printed in Poland
by Amazon Fulfillment
Poland Sp. z o.o., Wrocław

49380386R00026